GREEK
Oxi
('oh-hee)

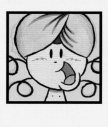

HINDI
Naheen

ETRUSCAN
Ein

HOPI INDIAN
Qa'e
('kah-eh)

JAPANESE
Iie
(iii-'yeh)

TIBETAN
Marey
(ma-'ray)

MONGOLIAN
Ügüi
(oo-'gwee)

OLD NORSE
Neinn

SKYWRITING

TIN CANS CONNECTED BY STRING

KOREAN
Aniyo
(a-nee-'oh)

COWBOY
Noooooope

TATTOO

PEAS

TEXT MESSAGE

SPANISH
(KIND OF)
No way, José

SEEK-'N'-FIND

SCOTTISH
Nae

VANITY PLATE

RUSSIAN
Nyet

Library of Congress Cataloging-in-Publication Data Warburton, Tom. 1000 times no / as told by Mr. Warburton. – 1st ed.   p.   cm.   Summary: When Noah's mother tells him that it is time to go, he finds more than a few ways to decline. ISBN 978-0-06-154263-3 (trade bdg.) — ISBN 978-0-06-154264-0 (lib. bdg.) [1. No (The English word)—Fiction.] I. Title. II. Title: One thousand times no.   PZ7.W185Aam 2009 2007044270 [E]—dc22 C|P AC

Typography by Sarah Hoy   1 2 3 4 5 6 7 8 9 10 ❖   First Edition

1000 TIMES NO

As told by Mr. Warburton

LAURA GERINGER BOOKS
AN IMPRINT OF HARPERCOLLINS PUBLISHERS

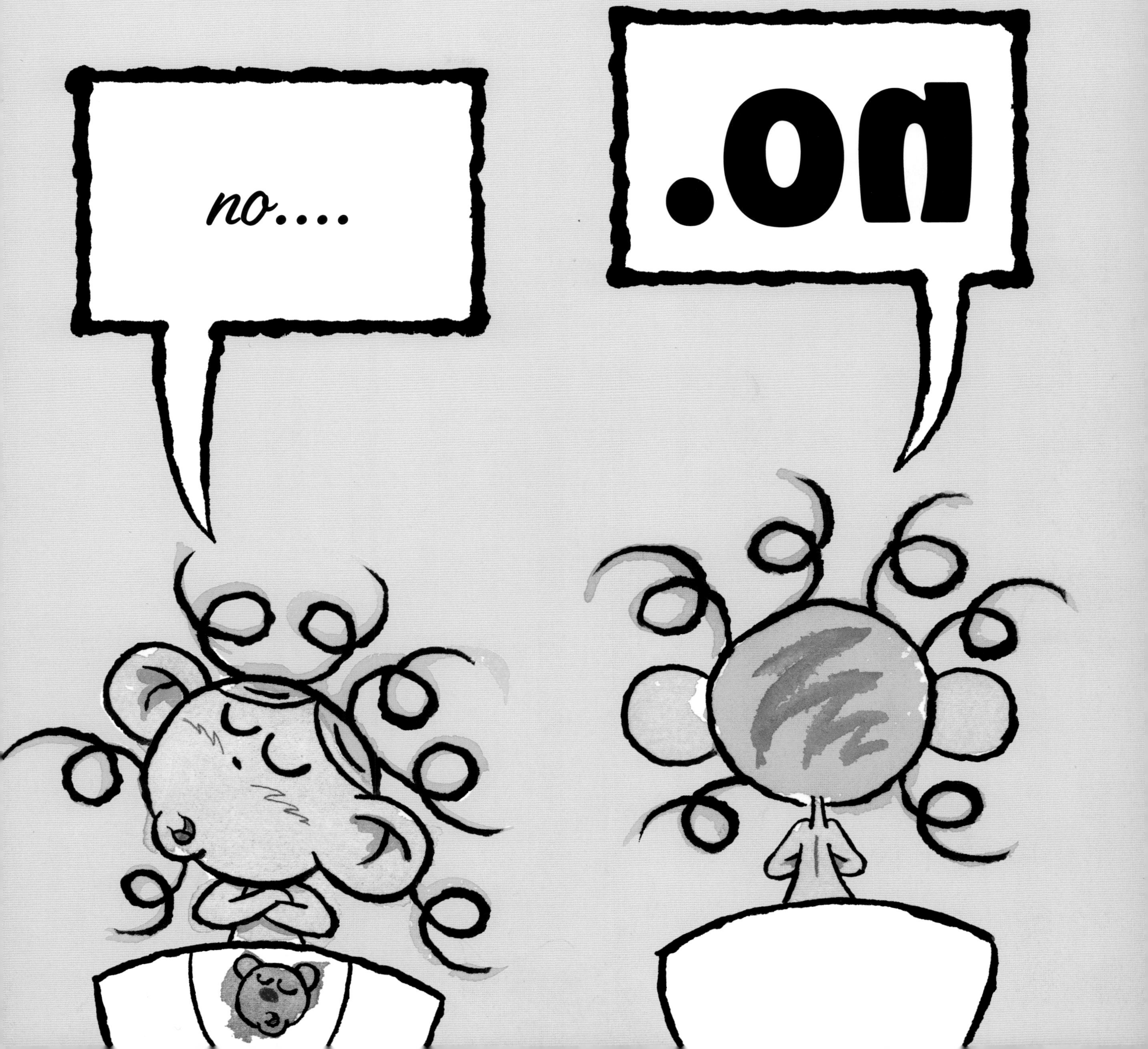
no....
no.

no.

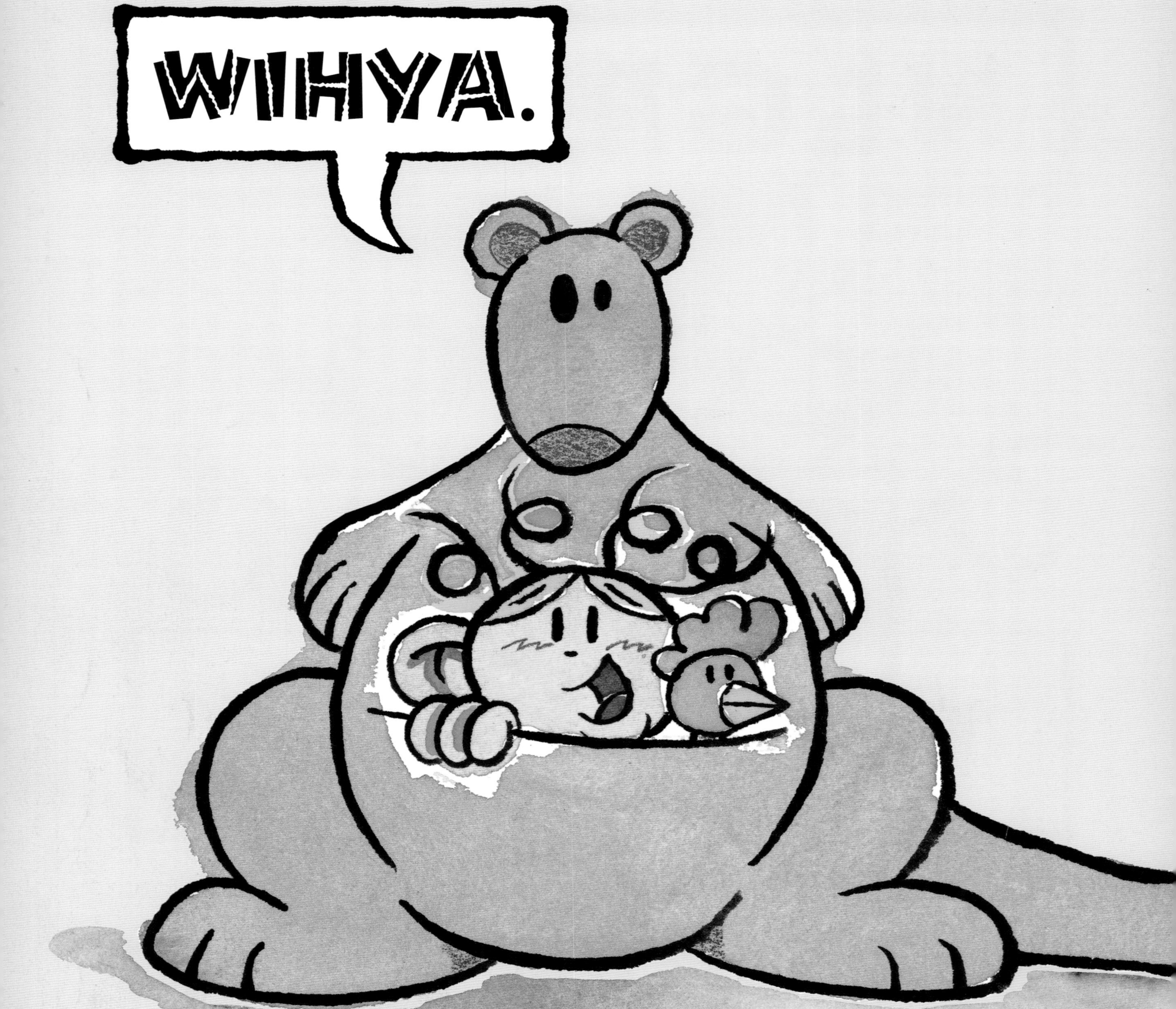
WIHYA.

ES!

THE END

 **COWBOY**
Noooooope

 **WAGIMAN**
(ABORIGINAL,
NORTHERN AUSTRALIA)
Wihya
(wih-'jah)

 **TAGALOG**
(PHILIPPINES)
Hindi po

 **DUTCH**
Nee
(Nay)

 **SPANISH**
(KIND OF)
No way, José

 **ZULU**
Tsha

 **HEAD
SHAKE**

 **MANDARIN
CHINESE**
Bu

 **RUSSIAN**
Nyet

 **ARABIC**
(USING EGYPTIAN
HIEROGLYPHICS)
Laa

 **INUIT**
(ESKIMO)
Naaga

 **HAWAIIAN**
'A'ole
(ah-'o-lay)

 **PIG LATIN**
O-nay

 **ALPHABET
BLOCKS**

 **LATIN**
Non

 **OSAGE
INDIAN**
Hon'-ka-zhi

 **ROBOT**
Negative

**AZTEC
INDIAN**
Amo

RAPANUI
(EASTER ISLAND)
Ina
('ee-nah)

   **MORSE
CODE**
Dah Dit–
Dah Dah Dah